Skate Park Swap

and other devos for guys on the go

Stephen Sorenson

Standard
Publishing

cincinnati, ohio

Contents

Unwilling to listen to advice and eager to show off a little, Jim breaks an important rule. Now much more is at stake, for him and everybody else.

Trapped!

"I'm tired of looking in these stores, Don," Jim complained to his brother. "I thought Cripple Creek would have more than just these souvenirs for tourists."

"Yeah, let's go exploring," Don said, hopping on his mountain bike. "When Dad finishes his meetings in Denver tomorrow, we're out of here."

"Where do you want to go?" Dennis asked his cousins as they started riding. "I know some good places."

"Let's go down here." Jim pedaled hard and started coasting down a hill. The other boys followed. After several blocks they turned onto a dirt road.

"There sure are lots of rocks," Don said as they passed a

huge mound of purple, yellow, and green-shaded rocks.

"How did miners get these rocks out of the ground?" Jim asked.

"Back in the early 1890s, they used picks, shovels, dynamite, donkeys, and sometimes carts on rails," Dennis replied. "Sometimes they built wooden braces called 'cribbing' to hold up their tunnels. Before electricity was brought in, miners cranked the ore buckets out by hand. By 1894, there were more than one hundred mines in this area. Most of the entrances are closed now."

"What's that?" Jim pointed.

"An ore chute. The miners sent ore down the chutes into wagons. After railroads began stopping here regularly, miners shoveled ore from the wagons into railroad cars to be shipped to processing mills."

Jim laid his bicycle down and began hiking up a rocky slope. "I'm going to explore. Are you coming?"

"OK." Dennis and Don followed him, but more slowly.

"I'm glad I didn't have to shovel all this rock," Don said.

"So am I." Dennis looked at the hills of tailings. "My father told me that a person loading ore into a wagon had to move more than thirty-five tons a day!"

When Dennis reached the top, he waited for Don, and they walked toward several old buildings.

"Jim, where are you?" Don called out.

"In here."

Dennis hurried toward the largest building. Its tin roof and log walls had partially collapsed. "Where are you?" Don asked again.

"Here." Jim's face popped up from underneath boards in a fenced-in area. "I'm exploring this mine shaft."

"Get out of there!" Dennis exclaimed. "It's dangerous."

"What's wrong?" Jim asked.

"That fence is here to keep people out. How'd you get over it?"

"I climbed." Jim grinned. "It's great down here. There are lots of old boards, an old pick, and a big hole in the center that looks like it goes into a room."

"Jim, get out of there!" Dennis ordered, trying to stay

calm. "Those boards are rotten, and the sides could cave in."

"You're just afraid to admit that you've never done this." Jim ducked back down. "I'm going to discover what's under here no matter what."

"Jim," Dennis' voice grew louder, "climb out. There are plenty of awesome places near here that aren't this danger-ous."

"He's right," Don said, putting his hand on the fence.

"I've climbed around old houses for years," Jim bragged, and the two boys could hear him moving boards. "I bet I know more about places like this than you do."

"Maybe," Dennis said, "although I've lived here all my life. You don't have to prove anything. Come out before you get hurt."

Jim's voice was muffled. "I'm glad I brought this flash-light."

Suddenly several boards fell in, and piles of dirt slid down. A cloud of dust rose. Jim cried out and then was silent.

"Are you OK?" Dennis shouted. He listened carefully and thought he heard a moan. He grabbed Don's arm. "Stay here in case he starts talking. If he does, tell him not to move. Do you understand?" Dennis looked Don in the eye. "And don't help him by yourself."

"OK." Don's voice wavered. "Will he be all right?"

"I don't know. I'll get help." Dennis scrambled to his bicycle and pedaled furiously to the sheriff's office. "Sheriff Douglas," he blurted out, breathing heavily, "my cousin is trapped in an old mine. He climbed down, and something happened."

"Which mine?"

"The first one on the hill, off the old Shelf Road."

The sheriff telephoned several people, then grabbed a flashlight and rope.

"My other cousin is there," Dennis added. "He'll show you where Jim is. I've got to tell my parents. I warned Jim, but he didn't listen."

"I'll handle things," the sheriff said.

Within minutes after Dennis got home, he and his parents were driving toward the mine. "Didn't you tell him not to go in there?" his mother asked.

"I didn't have time." Tears smudged Dennis' cheeks. "He

climbed up there first and went in before I could stop him. When I told him to get out, he wouldn't."

"I hope he's not too far down," his father said.

"I thought I heard him." Dennis replied. "He must be near the top."

"Thank God for that," his mother said. The three of them jumped out of the car; Don met them at the top of the slope.

"Two men wearing ropes climbed in," Don said, "and these guys are helping. Jim started talking just after you left. Dirt kept sliding into the hole every time he moved. I told him to be as still and quiet as he could." Don clenched his fists. "I wanted to help him but . . ."

"Jim wouldn't listen to me," Dennis repeated.

"You did the right thing," Mr. Riley reassured him. "Hand me the cell phone. I'll call your father right now."

"Jim wouldn't listen to me," Dennis repeated.

"It isn't your fault, Dennis." His mother hugged him. "You did what you could. Now it's up to these men. They're trained to do this." Her voice broke, and she looked away. A siren grew louder, and soon an ambulance drove up.

"How is Jim doing?" Mr. Riley asked a man holding a walkie-talkie.

"It could be much worse," the volunteer fireman replied. "His head is bleeding, and his leg is pinned under a beam. There's a lot of loose dirt over him, and the sheriff has tied a rope around his waist. As soon as we're sure nothing will fall on us, we'll get the beam off his leg."

Forty-five minutes later, rescuers hoisted Jim out of the shaft on a special backboard.

"May I ride with him to the hospital?" Mrs. Riley asked, holding Jim's hand. "He's my brother's son."

"Yes," an ambulance attendant said.

"He was lucky," the sheriff said as the ambulance left. "He nearly fell into the shaft."

"How deep is it?" Don asked. "A hundred feet?"

"More than a thousand."

After watching the firemen coil up a rope and repair the fence, Don said, "Maybe the fence should be higher."

"It probably wouldn't have made any difference." Sheriff Douglas sighed. "There's always somebody who ignores signs and climbs into a place like this. I'm just glad things worked out as well as they did this time."

Live It!

Every day you have to make many choices, and your decisions sometimes make a huge difference—to you or someone else. Choose ahead of time what kind of decisions you want to make, and when temptations come they will be easier to resist if you ask for God's help. And remember, besides listening to wise friends and family members, spend some time reading the Bible. God has lots of awesome things to teach you.

Read It!

"The way of a fool seems right to him, but a wise man listens to advice."– Proverbs 12:15

Pray About It!

Lord, sometimes I don't want to listen to advice. I want to do things my own way. I'm tempted to show off so I can prove that I'm not afraid, or that I'm part of the group. Help me realize it's good to be afraid sometimes and that I don't have to act one way when I feel very different on the inside. A real friend will accept me the way I am and tell me true things I need to hear. Please help me listen to wise advice, including what I read in the Bible.

A bit of a thrill seeker, Ken dreams of going out in a sailboat and finally gets his chance. But when he doesn't pay attention to his father's warning, Ken faces challenges too big to handle by himself.

Talked into Trouble

Ken Jamison hopped from rock to rock on the water's edge. Careful not to get his shoes wet, he picked up a piece of driftwood.

"There's a lot of driftwood around here." Startled, Ken turned around. "I saw you coming," a boy sitting on an overturned rowboat said. "You aren't from around here, are you?"

"You're right," Ken replied. "We're going to be here for three weeks."

"I'm going sailing now."

"You have a boat?" Ken asked. "I've always wanted to go sailing. Do you sail often?"

"My dad lets me take the boat out," the boy said proudly.

"My name's David. What's yours?"

"Ken."

"Are you renting the cottage?"

Ken nodded. "Yeah. We arrived yesterday."

"I've been waiting for wind like this," David said. "Want to see my boat?"

"Sure." Ken followed David down the wooden pier. "How many people can this boat carry?"

"Several," David replied.

"Can I go with you?" Ken asked cautiously.

"Sure, but I'm ready to leave."

"I'll be right back," Ken said. "I'll get a jacket." He ran back to the cottage.

"Where've you been?" his father asked, putting down a magazine.

"On the beach." Ken dashed into his room.

"What's the hurry?"

"A guy invited me to go sailing."

"You should wait until we rent a boat," Mr. Jamison said, looking out the large picture window. "It's too gusty to sail today."

"Aw, Dad, he knows a lot about sailing. He lives here all year."

"There will be a better day, I'm sure."

Ken sighed. "I'll get bored just walking along the beach."

"There's a lot to see there, if you are observant," his mother stated. "You could probably find a crab or starfish."

"I don't feel like doing that."

"Your mother and I are going into town in an hour or so. Want to come?"

"I guess so." Ken pushed the screen door open and watched the gray clouds swirl. *Who's afraid of a little wind?* he thought.

Who's afraid of a little wind? he thought.

"All set?" David asked impatiently when Ken walked onto the pier.

Ken watched the curling whitecaps sweep by. "I can't go with you. My father thinks it's a bad sailing day."

"Did he say you couldn't go?" David looked up.

"He didn't specifically tell me I couldn't go, but I know what he meant."

"What does he know about sailing?" David pointed.

"Untie that rope, will you?"

"He used to sail with friends," Ken answered.

"Don't worry," David stated confidently. "I know this area." A large wave dashed against a post, splashing the boys. "Besides, this will be fun."

Ken looked back toward the cottage. "Maybe we should go later."

"And miss a wind like this? No way! It's now or never. I can always go by myself."

"I want to go," Ken replied, "but—"

"Then untie that rope and climb in." David stuffed two life jackets into the cockpit. "We have to have these, or we can be fined. But we don't have to wear them."

"Give me one," Ken said. "I don't swim well."

"You won't need it today, and it's packed." David gave Ken a funny look. "Only losers wear them."

"All right, I won't wear it, but hand it to me anyway."

David tossed him the life preserver. "Just hold on and do what I tell you." As David raised the sails, they began to flap. "Lower the centerboard, Ken. It's deep enough."

"What's a centerboard?"

"This thing." David pointed. "Pull it toward you, and it'll go down. It helps to keep the boat from drifting sideways, and sometimes," he added, "it catches seaweed in shallow water." He passed a line through a cleat and put his right hand on the rudder.

"We're moving!" Ken exclaimed

"This boat is fast," David bragged.

"We won't stay out very long, will we?" Ken sat on a cushion. "I have to be back in an hour."

"No problem."

A large wave smacked into the boat; water splashed over the sides. "Whew, that water's cold."

"You'll get used to it," David said. "After a—" A gust of wind suddenly hit the sails. The boat heeled over precariously. "Move to the other side," David shouted.

Ken crawled over the centerboard and under the boom so quickly that he banged his knee. "Next time warn me, OK?"

"I'll try," David said. "See that plastic bucket? Bail out some water."

"Why'd the boat tip so much?"

David frowned. "It's not my fault this wind is so strong."

"You said it's good to sail when the wind is like this," Ken replied.

David licked salt spray off his lips. "It's stronger than I thought."

Suddenly the boom swung across the hull, nearly knocking Ken out of the boat and bruising his shoulder. David struggled to adjust the sail.

"You said you were a good sailor," Ken said as the boat again headed into the waves.

"**D**on't worry," David stated confidently. "I know this area."

"I go out sometimes," David said defensively. "I've just never gone out this far."

"How long have you had this boat?" Ken asked.

"Since March." David tightened his grip on the rudder. As the boat chopped into the whitecaps, water sprayed over the bow. "Isn't this fun?" David shouted. Ken began to shiver.

"Haven't we gone far enough?"

"We'll turn back soon," David said. The boat pitched up and down as the waves grew larger. "Watch how fast this boat turns. We're going to come about. When I tell you, move quickly to the other side. "OK, . . . move!" The sailboat turned just as another gust of wind hit the sails. The boom knocked Ken backward.

"Get to the other side," David yelled as a wave hit them broadside. Freezing water poured in. Ken fell overboard and gasped for air. David climbed as high as he could on the opposite side, trying to raise the sails out of the water. Seconds later, the mast began sinking.

"Climb on," David screamed, and Ken grabbed the mast.

"Not that way. Swim over here."

"I can't," Ken yelled, eyes wide with fear. Then David tumbled into the water.

Clinging to a life preserver, Ken tried to keep from being bruised as waves pounded the boat. The cold water numbed him; his clothing weighted him down. When the boat turned completely over, he tried desperately to hold onto the hull.

"Hold on!" someone shouted, and Ken heard an engine. Seconds later, his father pulled him into a large boat. He hunched over in the biting wind. Soon David sat beside him.

"What'll my dad say when he gets home?" David said,

his lips blue. "I wasn't supposed to take the boat out."

I sure was wrong about David, Ken thought. A large lump formed in his throat when his father wrapped him in a blanket. "I'm sorry," Ken said, his teeth clenched.

"We're lucky," his father said. "If I hadn't seen you get on the boat, and if the neighbor hadn't been home, I don't know what would have happened."

Live It!

It's fun to try new activities and push physical limits, but it's important to take nature into account, too. How can you find the balance between what's challenging and what's dangerous? God wants you to live a full life, but that means finding the right balance. And he encourages you to listen to the wisdom of those who are in authority over you. It's easy to think that they don't really understand, but they do. After all, they were your age once and know what it's like.

Read It!

"A wise son heeds his father's instruction."–Proverbs 13:1

Pray About It!

Lord, I thank you for the many fun things I can do. Help me to listen to what you say in the Bible and to what wise adults tell me. When I'm tempted to take risks just because somebody wants me to, please give me the strength to resist and to stand up for what's right. Thank you for people who care enough not to let me do dangerous things.

It's great to get a new gift, such as a bike or skateboard. But, as Stephen discovers, sharing a cool gift you want to keep for yourself can sometimes lead to special surprises.

Skate Park Swap

Mr. Yancey erased the chalkboard and turned to the seven boys in his Sunday school class. "Before the bell rings, I want to know how many of you would be interested in a weekend camping and skateboarding trip. We'd leave a week from Friday, right after school, and come home on Sunday evening."

"Then we'll miss church," Stephen said.

"Yes," Mr. Yancey replied, "but we'll have a Bible and prayer time wherever we are."

"But you won't have a chalkboard to draw pictures on," Douglas said.

"Maybe," Larry said, grinning, "we could take some chalk

and camp near a sidewalk."

"That's enough." Mr. Yancey looked at his watch. "First you have to decide if you'd like to go. If you do, you'll need to get this permission and medical release form signed by a parent or guardian."

"Where would we go?" asked Jason, a thin boy with dark hair.

"I know a great national forest campground near Denver," Mr. Yancey said, "and we'd go from there to one of the best skate parks in Denver. It's indoors and has great bowls, low-boxes, and transitions."

"Where would we sleep?" Stephen asked. "I don't even have a tent, just a summer sleeping bag. My parents don't like to camp,"

"I've got a big tent," Mr. Yancey said, "and a propane cooking stove."

"I'll go," Stephen said.

"How about you, Randy?" Mr. Yancey asked.

"Count me in."

"What about the rest of you?"

"I think the trip sounds cool," Tom said, looking at everyone, "but won't it cost lots of money?"

"Not as much as you'd think," Mr. Yancey answered. "Basically you just chip in for food and pay the skate park's entrance fee on Saturday. I'll drive my van." He paused. "I've worked out a way for you to earn the money you'll need. If you show up at church on Saturday morning about 9:00, you can help the church custodian do yard work."

"**I'm** not sure I can go," Ted stated.

"I'm not sure I can go," Tom stated.

"Why not?" Stephen asked. "Afraid I'll show you up in the park?" Tom's face clouded over, and immediately Stephen was sorry he'd said that. *Sometimes jokes end up hurting people,* he thought.

"Maybe things will work out somehow, Tom," Mr. Yancey said. "Anyway, we're out of time. Here are the permission slips. Give them to me by Sunday at the latest. And," he paused, "here's a basic list of what to bring."

"I'm glad we're doing this now," Al said. "If we waited longer, it might be too cold."

"What if it does get cold?" Randy asked. "I get cold easily."

"I have several extra sleeping bags if you need one," Mr. Yancey said. "But remember, what you take must fit in the van or in the rack outside. Keep to the list as much as possible, and this time the only music we'll have will be CDs in the van."

"You mean I'll have to listen to the birds and these guys in the campground?" Tony asked. "I don't think I can stand it."

"Then I guess you'll suffer a little," Mr. Yancey said, smiling. "Hey, don't forget to stack your chairs."

On Saturday, Mr. Yancey showed up to help the boys and brought three leaf rakes. "Has anybody talked with Tom to see if he's going camping and skating with us?"

"I don't think he really wants to come," Stephen said. "When I mentioned it at school yesterday, he said he'd probably stay home."

"Are you sure?" Al asked, piling up some leaves. "He's a fun guy to have along."

"I'll phone him tonight," Mr. Yancey said.

Later that evening, Mr. Yancey called Tom. "Can you come with us next weekend? Everyone else is going, and they were asking about you today."

"They were?" Tom paused. "I'd like to go, but I can't."

"Why not?"

"I . . . don't have a skateboard. Mine was stolen. But Dad is going to help me buy a new one once his new business gets going."

"Maybe we can work out something," Mr. Yancey said. "Maybe one of the guys has an extra skateboard."

"I don't want to be a bother," Tom replied. "Thanks for calling."

The next morning, everyone showed up for Sunday school but Tom. "Where is he?" Stephen asked. "Doesn't he want to know the plans?"

Mr. Yancey explained Tom's problem. "He doesn't want to ask anyone to lend him a skateboard."

"I don't have one to lend," Al stated, "and my brother sure wouldn't let anyone use his. It has top-notch bearings and wheels, so it goes really fast."

Mr. Yancey shook his head. "I really want Tom to be able to go with us. Maybe I can find one someplace."

That afternoon, Stephen sat down in his room. *I don't have a good skateboard to lend Tom*, he thought, *since my old one just has cheap bearings and is pretty worn out. And my new one gets here on Wednesday, and I don't want to lend that to anyone.* He smiled as he thought about the new skateboard he had helped his parents pick out for his birthday. *It'll sure be better than that old one, and the 53-millimeter wheels will give me more grind clearance.*

He walked into his room and looked at his old

> **"I** could lend you my new skateboard. It arrives on Wednesday."

skateboard. *I could lend this one to Tom,* he thought. But the longer Stephen looked at it, the more he realized that it would be too small for Tom. *He's way taller than I am, and this is nearly too small for me. He will want a wider board for the park, just like me.*

Stephen walked outside and stood near the street. *But what if something happens to my new skateboard? During our fishing trip in July, Tom dropped the cooler and cracked it.*

Finally Stephen telephoned Tom. "Hey, if you want to go with us," he said, choosing his words carefully, "I could lend you my new skateboard. It arrives on Wednesday."

"What'll you ride if you do that?" Tom replied, surprised.

"My old one. It'd be too small for you."

"Yours must have cost a lot," Tom exclaimed. "Are you sure you want to do that?"

Stephen suddenly realized he really did want to do that. "That's what friends are for."

"It's hard for me to accept, but I will," Tom said, "on one condition. I want to give you something in return."

"What?"

"You mentioned you don't have a tent, and I have three of them now. A neighbor who used to be a Boy Scout leader was moving and gave me two dome tents. I'd like you to have one. Is it a deal?"

"OK," Stephen agreed, "but it sounds like I'm getting the best deal of all."

Tom laughed. "Somebody once told me that's what friendship is all about. Aren't surprises fun?"

Live It!

Many kids today get their identities in what they have—shoes, skateboards, clothes, and other things. But if you are a Christian, you have much more than just *things*. You have God in your life, who loves you and wants to provide for your needs. It's not easy to find the right balance between owning things and having things own you. But with God's help, you can find that balance. Take a look at how you view your things. Do you share them? Do you help other kids who are in need? Do you tell other kids how awesome God is and share the Bible with them? So many kids all around you don't know anything about God and the Bible. What a great opportunity you have to share!

Read It!

"And do not forget to do good and to share with others, for with such sacrifices God is pleased."–Hebrews 13:16

Pray About It!

Dear Lord, it's so easy to get too attached to things I really like. Help me to be willing to share what I have, and to act responsibly with everything you've given to me. I want to be less selfish and more generous and loving so that people around me will be drawn to you. Thank you for letting me talk with you, and for really listening.

When Timothy leaves for school, he has no idea that something he will do later will make him feel guilty and miserable. The choices he makes will reveal a lot about the kind of boy he really is.

Nobody Knows

"How's it going, Timothy?" asked Mrs. Mitchell, the sixth grade teacher. "You've been here a week, and you seem to fit in just fine."

"I like it here," Timothy said slowly. "Kids are pretty friendly, and I left my ruler on my desk and nobody stole it."

Mrs. Mitchell chuckled. "Students take pride in this school. Are you all moved in?"

"Mostly," Timothy answered, "but we're still unpacking."

"Don't let me delay you," Mrs. Mitchell said. "I just want you to know I'm glad you're in my class."

"Thanks." Timothy's heavy backpack cut into his shoulders as he hurried home. *I wonder what Phil would say if he saw these?* he thought, looking at the tall oak trees. *In Chicago we had to go to a park to see trees like this. But I miss my friends in the apartment building.*

A loud bark interrupted his thoughts. Used to stray dogs, he picked up a rock without even thinking about it. *Yesterday Josh warned me about an old lady's mean dog near here that chased him down the street.*

A block farther, Timothy threw his rock at a squirrel on a telephone wire. The rock just missed the squirrel and flew over a blossoming hedge. Then a loud bang startled him.

What did it hit? Timothy peered through the hedge. His rock lay on the hood of an older car. *I hit the car!* He crouched down so nobody would see him. *I've got to get out of here before I get caught.* He cut across the street and started running.

"I've got to get out of here before I get caught."

Breathless, he opened the front door. "I'm home, Mom."

"How was school? How come you're out of breath?"

"I ran partway," Timothy answered, wiping his forehead.

"Well, change clothes. I need help unpacking before you do homework."

I didn't mean to hit the car, Timothy thought as he carried a box. *Did someone follow me home?*

During dinner his sister, Sarah, kept giving him strange looks. Finally she asked, "Are you feeling OK? You sure are quiet."

"And," his father added, "you haven't had seconds on potatoes."

Just then the telephone rang, and his mother picked up the receiver. Timothy stiffened. *Maybe somebody is reporting me.* He sighed with relief when it was someone who welcomed families that just moved into town.

Timothy's heart beat quickly. Did Dad find out?

That evening, he couldn't concentrate on his spelling homework. *Maybe the rock didn't dent anything,* he thought, *and it isn't my fault the car was hidden.*

"Timothy, want to sample your sister's brownies?"

Startled, Timothy turned around. "I didn't hear you knock."

"Your door was open." His mother looked at him carefully. "Are you sure you're all right?"

"I'm tired." Timothy forced a smile.

"Well, you've been tired plenty of times, and you haven't acted like this. Maybe brownies will cheer you up."

"I put in extra nuts just for you," Sarah said as he entered the kitchen.

"Thanks." Timothy stuffed a brownie into his mouth.

"Are they good?" his sister asked.

"They're OK."

"Just OK? I thought they were your favorite, and I made them just for you."

"Cut it out, will you? I said they were OK."

Sarah made a face. "You sure are crabby. That's the last time I'll make brownies for you."

Timothy had nearly reached the stairs when his father said, "I'd like to talk with you, Timothy."

Timothy's heart beat quickly. *Did Dad find out?*

"You are making everybody miserable," Mr. Franklin said. "Would you mind telling me what's wrong?"

"I can't," Timothy said, squirming.

His father looked him in the eye. "Your sister was only trying to cheer you up."

"I didn't mean to say those things to her." Timothy

walked into the kitchen. "I'm sorry, Sarah. The brownies were great, and I'm not just saying that."

Sarah's face brightened. "I did the best I could. Mom's teaching me."

That night it took Timothy a long time to fall sleep. He woke up once in the night, sweating, after dreaming somebody was chasing him.

"Breakfast is on the table," his mother said when she woke him up. "Your father is in the garage and needs your help soon."

After breakfast Timothy walked outside. His father was arranging tools on a sheet of pegboard. "How are you, Timothy?"

"I had a hard time sleeping," Timothy replied. "Dad, have you ever had something happen that wasn't really your fault and yet it was?"

"I'm not sure what you mean."

"Have you ever done something bad by accident and had to tell someone you did it?"

"Yes. During high school I worked for a man doing yard work. One afternoon I had to back his car out of his narrow garage to wash it, but he had left the wheels a little crooked. When I backed out, I knocked off some chrome. So I had to tell him."

"Dad, can I leave for a while?"

"I guess so. Is there something I can help with?"

"Not this time." Timothy stood up. "I have to do this myself. I'll be back as soon as I can."

Timothy walked to where he had thrown the rock. *Why not forget about the whole thing?* a small voice told him. *Why confess now?*

He hesitated, then walked up the driveway. Suddenly a German shepherd bounded up, barking fiercely.

"What do you want?" an older woman asked, opening her front door. "King, be still!" The dog stopped barking and eyed Timothy.

"Do you live here?" Timothy asked, feeling stupid because she probably did.

"Yes. If you're selling candy for the school band, you're too late. I just bought two boxes."

Timothy's throat was dry. "I came to tell you something."

"Come in." The woman smiled. "King is friendly, once he knows you."

Not convinced, Timothy kept watching the dog, which followed him.

"What can I do for you?" the woman asked. "My name is Mrs. Randall."

"I'm Timothy," he blurted out. "I'm sorry I hit your car with a rock. I was trying to hit a squirrel."

"I saw the rock. I thought another kid threw it . . . the one who teases King and put big rocks on my driveway. Last time King chased him away."

"I didn't mean to hit your car," Timothy said.

"I didn't mean to hit your car," Timothy said.

"I'm sure you didn't," replied Mrs. Randall, "but it scratched the hood."

"Last night," Timothy continued, "I tried to forget I threw the rock, but I couldn't."

"So you came here to make things right?"

Timothy nodded. "But I don't have much money."

"Well, I forgive you. Let's look at the car. If it's something I should get fixed, maybe we can work out a deal. Maybe you can help me do chores."

Timothy felt so relieved he almost laughed for no reason.

As they walked outside, King brushed against Timothy's leg. *So this is the mean dog Josh told me about,* he thought. *A new guy like me has a lot to learn.*

Live It!

It takes courage to admit you've hurt someone, ask him or her for forgiveness, and make things right. But you can, with God's help. You can experience the joy that comes from not carrying around guilt. In fact, Jesus died on the cross and rose from the dead so your sins could be forgiven. If you haven't already, give your life to Jesus and ask him to forgive your sins. He will do it! Remember, everybody makes mistakes. It's what you do afterward that really counts.

Read It!

"Be kind and compassionate to one another, forgiving each other, just as in Christ God forgave you." –Ephesians 4:32

Pray About It!

Dear Lord, please give me the courage to admit to you and other people when I do wrong things, and then ask for forgiveness. And help me to forgive kids who hurt me instead of trying to get back at them. I don't want to ignore my conscience when I do wrong. Make me aware of ways in which I hurt people, even by accident. I want to face my sin and become more like Jesus. Thanks for forgiving me when I confess what I've done to you. It feels so good to be forgiven.

It's easy to get sidetracked and choose not to keep a promise. Jimmy learns a hard lesson about this—one he won't quickly forget.

Jimmy Makes a Promise

"Jimmy and Susan, get your coats and boots on. We're going to Eagle River to buy snacks for the party tonight."

Jimmy looked up. "Do I have to go, Dad? Lots of kids are going ice-skating in half an hour, and I'd like to go. They're meeting at the lodge."

"I want to go skating, too," six-year-old Susan said.

"Are any adults going?" Mr. Hardy asked.

"Yeah. Pastor Stevens and some Sunday school teachers."

"Will anyone Susan's age be going? You know she can't keep up with you and your friends."

"I'm sure somebody she knows is going," Jimmy said eagerly.

"All right, Jimmy," Mrs. Hardy said. "We'll leave you in charge. Dress warmly, and stay with the group. Remember, Susan gets cold easily. Take good care of her."

"I will," Jimmy promised.

Moments later, Jimmy looked out at the lake as his parents drove away. *I wish we had places like this back home,* he thought. *Maybe our church could come here for a week next year instead of just a weekend.*

"Are you ready, Susan?" Jimmy called out.

"I can't find my mittens." Susan frowned.

"I'll help you as soon as I get my skates."

Taking care of Susan won't be hard, he thought. *She'll find somebody to skate with. I just hope she doesn't get in the way.*

"Jimmy, I found them. They were under this coat. Will you play ice tag with me?" Susan's eyes sparkled. "Remember when we did that at Herrick's Lake?"

"That was a while ago," Jimmy said slowly. "Now I like to race."

Taking care of Susan won't be hard, he thought.

"Why won't you race with me anymore?"

"I like to do things with kids my own age," Jimmy replied, opening the door.

They walked along the snow-tromped path to the lodge. As they entered the doorway, Jimmy's friend Paul called out, "Jimmy, we're going to play broom hockey today."

"Great!" " Jimmy unzipped his coat. "See anybody your age, Susan?"

"I'll find someone," Susan said. "I'm big enough to take care of myself." She walked over to some girls.

"Well, that solves that problem," Jimmy said, turning to Paul. "I didn't want to baby-sit her anyway."

With Pastor Stevens in the lead, the group left the lodge, brooms in hand. They crossed several paths and stopped once to make sure they were still on the correct one.

"Look how smooth the ice is," Paul said as they approached the pond.

Jimmy laced up his skates quickly. "I haven't skated since last year. It's much colder this year."

Paul tucked his scarf around his neck. "Yeah. This wind cuts right through you."

"We'll warm up quickly." Jimmy stepped onto the ice.

"Hey, I still remember how to skate backward." He skated in a circle, and his skate blades cut into the ice when he stopped.

"Jimmy." Susan's voice carried in the wind.

"I wonder what she wants," Jimmy said. "I'd better go see." He skated over to the bank. "What's wrong?"

"I can't get my skate on," Susan complained.

"Hey, that's not the way to do it. Loosen all the laces, not just the ones at the top." Jimmy picked up her other skate and loosened the laces. "Try this one." Susan put her foot into the skate. "Good." Jimmy stood up. "Now do the other one like that. I'll be with Paul and some other guys."

"What about me?" Susan asked.

"Skate with the girls," Jimmy said.

After playing broom hockey for about an hour, the boys started racing. As Jimmy lined up to race Paul, Susan skated up. Her ankles were bent out to the sides, and her face was bright red. "Jimmy, I'm freezing. Let's go back."

"Not yet."

"But my ankles hurt," Susan complained, "and I want to leave now. I told the girls I'd walk back with you. Maybe I can catch up with them."

"Go ahead. I'll come later."

The boys kept skating, and the wind became more gusty.

"Boy, are my toes cold!" Paul exclaimed.

"Mine too." Jimmy stamped his skates on the ice. "Let's quit." The other four boys agreed.

Paul skated to the far bank, and Jimmy followed. "Where's your sister?"

"She left a while ago."

Paul pulled up his collar. "Let's go."

About halfway back to the cabins, the bitterly cold wind began to make Jimmy's eyes water. "Are we still on the right path, Paul?"

Paul studied the surroundings. "Yes. I remember that stump."

Soon they reached the parking lot. "See you later," Jimmy said. "I need to check on my sister." He walked along the shoreline and opened the cabin door. "Hey, Susan, how're you doing?" When she didn't answer, Jimmy added, "This is no time to hide. Where are you?" Unable to find her,

Jimmy walked back to the lodge where people were sitting around the fireplace.

"Pastor Stevens, have you seen my sister? I last saw her at the pond."

"No." He turned to several girls. "Did any of you walk back with Susan Hardy?"

"I saw her cross the pond as I put on my boots," one girl said, "but we didn't wait for her. She said she'd go with her brother."

Pastor Stevens turned to Jimmy. "Did she say anything to you before she left?"

"That she was cold, so I told her to go back."

"Was she alone when she left?"

"I don't know," Jimmy said.

"Maybe she's with your parents."

"No, they went to town."

"Then we'd better find her." Pastor Stevens called to several parents. "Hey, Jimmy's sister isn't back from the pond, so we need to look for her." He looked at Jimmy. "Wait at your cabin and warm up. When we find your sister, we'll bring her over."

As Jimmy trudged back to the cabin, his mother's words kept running through his mind. "Take good care of her." Jimmy sat down heavily in the couch and prayed. "Lord, please take care of Susan. I was supposed to watch out for her, but I didn't. I don't want anything bad to happen to her. "

Jimmy thought about the fun times he'd had with Susan, and how much he secretly enjoyed her questions. The wind rattled a branch against the window.

Soon he heard footsteps on the porch, and the door opened. "Hey, Susan . . ." Jimmy stopped talking when he saw his father in the doorway.

"How was the skating?" Mr. Hardy asked cheerfully.

Mrs. Hardy looked at Jimmy. "What's wrong? Lose all your races?"

As Jimmy began to tell what had happened, someone knocked. Mr. Hardy opened the door,

"Mr. Hardy?" a man asked.

"Yes."

"My name is Bill Peterson, and I work for the camp."

"Want to come in, Bill?"

"Thank you. I just talked with your daughter. She's OK

and on her way back to camp now."

"Where was she? What do you mean she's OK?" Mrs. Hardy's voice rose.

"She was at Jacobsen's cabin, just south of here. She knocked on their door about an hour ago after wandering in the woods. They warmed her by the woodstove and are driving her back." Bill put on his hat and left.

"I'm sorry," Jimmy said slowly. "Once I started skating, I didn't pay much attention to Susan." When he finished describing what happened, his parents sat quietly for a moment. Then his father said, "We know you are sorry, and we want you to apologize to Susan. But," Mr. Hardy said gently, "before she gets here, I want to tell you about when I promised to care for my brother one day and got sidetracked. You aren't the only one who has had to learn a hard lesson about this kind of thing."

"Once I started skating, I didn't pay much attention to Susan."

He put his arm around Jimmy's shoulder.

Live It!

It's easy to get caught up in your own interests and neglect other people who need your help. This week, try an experiment. Every day, ask God to help you be compassionate, kind, humble, gentle, and patient. And every night think about what happened. God wants to help you be the best person you can be!

Read It!

"Whoever can be trusted with very little can also be trusted with much, and whoever is dishonest with very little will also be dishonest with much."–Luke 16:10

Pray About It

Lord, thank you for being willing to forgive me when I'm selfish and think of myself first. Help me to be kind and patient with my family and friends, and to always keep the promises I make.

As Lance struggles to be as good in athletics as other kids, his world seems to be coming apart. But much more is happening on the inside than he realizes.

Hidden Talents

Mr. Turner held up his hand. "On your mark, get set, go!" Six boys and girls dashed toward the finish line, kicking soccer balls as classmates cheered them on.

Tony turned to Lance. "We won't beat Miss Stockwell's class unless we do well now."

Lance nodded. "Yeah. When Mr. Turner suggested that we compete against the other class, I thought it was a dumb idea. But it's fun." He watched as his twin sister cheered for her class. "Jennifer will be really hoarse tonight."

"Are you ready to go?" Tony asked. "We're next."

"I guess so." Lance shaded his eyes against the sun. "It looks like Pete and Larry got first and second place in the ball race. That means we're about tied." He rolled up his sleeves and tightened his shoelaces.

"All right," Mr. Turner said, looking at the six pairs of students. "This is the last event. Stand next to your partner, and we'll tie one person's right leg to the other's left leg with a short piece of rope. When I blow the whistle, run around that tree where Miss Stockwell is standing and race back. If you fall, get up and keep going. First pair to cross this line wins."

"Do we have to go all the way across the finish line to win or just have an arm across it?" Tony asked.

"Each pair has to cross it completely," Mr. Turner replied.

Moments later the twelve students stood on the starting line. "Come on, Tony," a girl with glasses shouted when the whistle blew. "You can do it! The other class is just two points ahead."

"Faster," another girl yelled. "They're gaining on you!" Lance and Tony tried to run in unison.

This isn't easy, Lance thought. He took larger steps, forcing Tony to go faster.

"Hey, my legs aren't as long as yours," Tony said. "Slow down."

"Sorry," Lance replied.

Several pairs of students were ahead of Lance and Tony, but the two friends were gaining as they went around the tree. "Even if Larry and Mike come in second and we come in third," Lance said, breathing hard, "our class will win." He turned to look at how his sister was doing and tripped. By the time they untangled themselves and picked up their sunglasses, everybody else was way ahead. A minute later, they crossed the finish line in last place.

"We lost because of you guys," Ryan said, walking over to Lance and Tony.

"We lost because of you guys," Ryan said, walking over to Lance and Tony.

"I'm glad you're so great," Tony replied sarcastically. "Maybe everyone should be like you."

"We did better than you," Ryan said. "Scott and I finished first in our races." He walked closer to Lance. "If you didn't trip over your own feet, you'd do better. Why did you even enter this event?"

Lance didn't answer; he just looked the other way.

"You didn't have to say that," Tony said. "Who do you

think you are, anyway? The greatest athlete in the world?"

"At least I don't have skinny legs like Lance," Ryan said.

The school bell rang, and Mr. Turner blew his whistle. "That's it. Miss Stockwell's class won by six points." Several girls cheered.

As Lance walked slowly toward the gym, a short boy approached him and said, "I heard what Ryan said. Don't let it bother you. He thinks he's the greatest and has to tell everybody. I heard that he lives with his grandparents because his mother drinks too much."

"But he's right," Lance muttered. "I do trip over my own feet."

"Nobody's perfect," the boy said. "Besides, you're the best writer in our class."

"Being good in writing doesn't win races." Lance yanked open the heavy door. "I let our class down. But thanks anyway."

Later that afternoon, as Lance entered the living room, his sister exclaimed, "We beat you! Did you see how fast JoAnn and I were? I didn't ride the bus because Karen's sister gave me a ride home."

"How'd you do in the races, Lance?" their brother, Gary, asked.

"He fell down," Jennifer said, "so my class won."

"I asked Lance," Gary said.

"She's right. My class was doing well until I tripped," Lance said, his words dripping with discouragement.

"You can't help it if you're uncoordinated," Jennifer said.

"Jennifer, that wasn't a nice thing to say," Mrs. Stone commented as she entered the room.

"I wasn't being mean," Jennifer countered. "It's true. It isn't his fault."

Lance hurried to his room. *She's right,* he thought. *I'm no good in sports. Why should I keep trying? Why can't I be like Ryan? He can do everything.* Lance looked down at his skinny legs. *I'll never be that good.*

"Can I come in?" Gary asked.

"Yeah."

"I just wanted to tell you," Gary said, "that I know what it's like to try your hardest and still blow it."

"How could you know?" Lance retorted. "You're already on the first-string football team, and you do well in track."

"But when I was your age," Gary stated, "I seldom hit a pitch, and I dribbled a basketball so high that people always stole it. Don't you remember?"

"So what'd you do?"

"I felt sorry for myself and was jealous of the other guys, especially Jim Kressling. Then the gym teacher helped me realize that my body was growing so fast that I couldn't expect to be coordinated all at once. I gave myself time to improve and started working out."

"But what if I don't improve? I may not be like you when I get bigger."

Gary grinned. "I'm sure you won't be just like me. You're already taller and stronger than I was three years ago." He paused. "There's a lot more to life than being good at sports. You're a lot better than I'll ever be in other things."

"There's a lot more to life than being good at sports."

"Like what?"

"Like repairing things and writing and science," Gary answered. "But you won't do as well if you keep feeling sorry for yourself. Just use the talents you've been given and be thankful for who you are. Be patient with yourself. I have to keep reminding myself to do this, too."

"But people laugh at me whenever I play sports," Lance protested.

"So what? Do your best—that's what counts. Sometimes it seems like it, but winning isn't everything! You'll get other chances to do better. Believe in yourself, and get advice from the coaches. You've got lots going for you." He slapped Lance's shoulder playfully.

Lance stood up. "Want to play football with me sometime and teach me some moves?"

"How about after dinner tonight?" Gary asked. "I promise not to laugh at you for more than 10 minutes."

"You'd better not," Lance said, a smile spreading across his face.

Live It!

It's not easy when other kids are better than you in certain things. But God has made each of us unique, and that means you are gifted in a different way. Take the time to explore new things. Even if you fail, you might still have fun trying them. You may even discover a hidden talent you didn't know you had! If kids tease you, just admit that it hurts and find some friends who accept you the way you are. And remember to talk to God about what's happening in your life. He loves you just the way you are, and he's closer than you may imagine.

Read It!

"We have different gifts, according to the grace given us."–Romans 12:6

Pray About It!

Lord, I try so hard, but I'm just not as good at some things as other kids are. Help me to realize that's OK. You created me just the way I am, with other abilities they don't recognize. Deep inside I want to do my best and become the person you want me to be. Help me to be patient with myself as I grow and learn. And enable me to love kids who are unkind to me, just as Jesus loved people who mistreated him.

Placed in a difficult situation because of his friend, Kevin has to choose between going along with the crowd or standing up for what's right.

Guilty by Association

It was nearly noon when the two boys paused in front of Mason's Hobby Store. "Hey, let's go in here," Kevin said. "I want to buy a video game."

"OK," Jeff answered, "but we can't stay long. My brother said he'd take us skating after lunch."

The boys walked down the center aisle, glancing at sale items. Then Kevin stopped by the video games. "I want to buy this one," he said.

"Let me see it," Jeff replied. As Kevin handed him the box, Jeff slipped it under his jacket.

"What are you doing?" Kevin asked. "I have to take it to the cashier."

"No you don't," Jeff stated, a grin spreading across his face. "You won't even have to pay for it."

Kevin stared at Jeff in disbelief. "You're going to steal it?"

Kevin stared at Jeff in disbelief. "You're going to steal it?"

"Hey, don't talk so loud." Jeff looked up and down the aisle, and then said, "Sure. Everybody does it."

Kevin's heart beat faster. "I don't," he said. "Put it back."

"Don't worry," Jeff said. "There's just that one lady, and she's a customer. Nobody will know. Besides, the store won't miss it anyway."

"You shouldn't steal it," Kevin answered.

"I won't get caught. I've done this with other kids, and nobody has gotten caught." Jeff headed confidently for the front door; Kevin trailed behind, not sure what to do.

Suddenly the woman who had been in the next aisle rushed past Kevin and blocked the front door. "That's far enough, boys," she said. "I'm with store security. Come with me."

For a moment Jeff looked as if he would try to run out the door anyway, but the woman's look stopped him. "Yeah," he finally said, "but we haven't done anything."

The woman followed them closely. When they reached the back of the store, she said, "Now go through here."

Jeff pushed open the door, and a man behind a desk stood up. "I'm Harry Mason, the owner," he said. "Sit next to the wall." After the boys sat down, he continued, "Mrs. Olson is a security guard. Do you have something in your pockets that isn't yours? Please lay everything on the floor."

Kevin quickly pulled out his wallet and a comb, but Jeff hesitated. "Why do I have to do this?" he asked.

"Please unzip your jacket," Mr. Mason said firmly.

Jeff unzipped the jacket slowly, a frightened look in his eyes. "Now what?"

"Hold open the sides."

Jeff pulled the jacket open, and Mr. Mason saw the video game tucked into the large inside pocket. "Give that to me. I've already called the police, and you are on videotape."

"They won't call my mother, will they?" Jeff asked, gripping the sides of his chair. "I didn't mean to take the game, and I'll put it back!"

"You should have thought of that before you took it," Mr.

Mason said. Turning to Mrs. Olson, he added, "I'll watch them until the police arrive."

"I don't think he can do much to us," Jeff whispered to Kevin.

"Sit still and be quiet," Mr. Mason said.

Minutes later, a policeman entered the room. "I'm Officer Keyser," he said, looking at the boys. "What's the problem?"

"My security guard caught this blond boy stealing this video game," Mr. Mason replied. "He hid it under his jacket and was going out the door. The other boy was behind him."

> "My security guard caught this blond boy stealing this video game," Mr. Mason replied.

"But Kevin didn't do anything," Jeff stated.

"What's your name?" Officer Keyser asked Jeff, "and where do you live?"

"Jeff Schrader. I live at 1015 Fontmore Road."

"You live with your parents?"

"Just Mom. She's working at Dibble's."

As Officer Keyser picked up the telephone, Jeff stood up.

"You're not calling Mom, are you?"

"I have to inform your mother and your friend's parents," Officer Keyser said, holding the receiver up to his ear. "Hello, Mrs. Schrader? This is Officer Keyser with the Upton Police Department. Your son is being detained for shoplifting at Mason's, and I'd like you to come here right away." After he hung up, the policeman turned to Kevin. "I need to call your mom or dad, too. Although it appears you didn't shoplift, you were still with Jeff."

"I'm Kevin Walker, and I live at 4595 Meadowlane."

After talking with Kevin's father, Officer Keyser turned to the boys. "I'll wait until your parents get here before proceeding further. But I want you to know that you're in big trouble, Jeff."

Looking confused, Mrs. Schrader and Mr. Walker entered the room about the same time.

"Now," Officer Keyser said, "where did you hide the video game, Jeff?"

"In my jacket pocket," Jeff said quietly, his face turning red. "But I didn't take it outside the store."

"If you conceal a product on your person inside the

store, the law says you are guilty of shoplifting."

"But it's just a video game," Jeff replied. "What's the big deal?"

"Well," Officer Keyser said, "shoplifting is a misdemeanor crime. I'm giving you a summons, which your mother will have to sign, showing the date when you will appear before a judge in municipal court. But we're letting you off easy. We could send you to the youth detention center."

A tear trickled down Jeff's cheek.

After Officer Keyser completed Jeff's summons, Mrs. Schrader asked, "When can we go?"

"As soon as you sign the summons," he replied. "Be sure Jeff shows up for his court date."

"Oh, my!" Mrs. Schrader exclaimed. "You weren't just bluffing."

"No," Officer Keyser said. "This store prosecutes shoplifters, just like the sign in the front window says."

"But he's only 12 years old. Can they do that?" She took a pen out of her purse and signed the summons.

"Yes," Officer Keyser said. "Now it's up to the judge, who will hear what Jeff has to say. The judge may order Jeff to pay a fine and do hours of community service, for example. You can take him home now, but make sure he appears in court."

After Jeff and his mother left, Kevin turned to Officer Keyser. "I didn't steal anything, and I didn't want Jeff to steal."

"Maybe so," Officer Keyser said, "but if things had been a little different I might have had to give you a summons. I wanted you to hear this, understand how serious shoplifting is, and think about the friends you hang around with. I've seen kids drawn into terrible situations."

"I do understand it," Kevin said, sweating.

"You may go."

"I'm proud of you for standing up for what was right," Kevin's father said as they left the store. "Now, how are you going to deal with Jeff?"

"Well," Kevin replied, "I still want to be his friend, but . . ."

Live It!

Some kids pressure their friends to do wrong things. If that happens to you, how will you respond? Although you can choose friends wisely, bad situations will still occur. If you decide ahead of time how you will respond, it'll be easier to resist the temptation to give in when a bad situation suddenly arises. Remember, too, that God is always with you and will give you the strength to stand up for what's right.

Read It!

"He who walks with the wise grows wise, but a companion of fools suffers harm."—Proverbs 13:20

Pray About It!

Lord, please help me stay away from kids who try to get me to do wrong things. I know how easy it can be to go along with them. Thank you for your willingness to help me stand up for what's right. Lead me to friends who want to obey you. And whenever I blow it and end up making a wrong choice, help me to confess my sins and make things right again.

Do you have an elderly grandparent, or know an elderly person in your neighborhood or church? Todd is about to discover just how cool an older person can be.

Grandpa Comes to Stay

Randy ambled across the street. "Hey, what's up?"

"Hi," Todd answered, laying down the dandelion digger. "How was your vacation?"

"Well," Randy began, "our visit at Grandpa's wasn't fun."

"Why not?"

"Grandpa lives in an old apartment. The rooms smell like stale onions, and Dad wouldn't let me play outside because I wasn't familiar with the city."

"So you just sat around?" Todd asked.

"Yep. All Grandpa wanted to do was tell the same boring stories over and over."

"What else did you do?"

"We went out to dinner," Randy said, "but Grandpa choked on a piece of meat and some guy had to grab him around his stomach to get it out. After that, Grandpa wasn't hungry and wanted to go home."

Todd wiped sweat off his forehead. "I'd better get back to work. Sorry about your trip."

"I guess that's what happens when people get old." Randy shrugged his shoulders.

"My grandpa from Texas is coming to stay with us," Todd said. "Just after you left, Mom told us. She doesn't want him in a nursing home. Dad's picking him up at the airport now."

"I hope it works out." Randy made a face. "Old people aren't any fun. They just need everybody to do things for them." He turned around when he reached the curb. "Hey, there's a kite contest in Memorial Park on Sunday afternoon. They'll judge the kites on the way they're made and how high they fly."

"Sweet," Todd said. "Want to enter?"

"Sure. Come over about 8:00 tomorrow morning."

"OK." Todd continued digging up weeds. *If Grandpa Willy is anything like Randy's grandpa, I hope he doesn't stay long,* he thought. When he finished, he stuffed the weeds into the garbage can.

"Could you help me?" Mrs. Stone looked up from the kitchen table as Todd came in. "I need you to clean the bathroom Grandpa Willy will use."

If Grandpa Willy is anything like Randy's grandpa, I hope he doesn't stay long, he thought.

"Yeah." Todd yanked open the cupboard door and took out a sponge and cleanser.

"What's wrong?"

"Nothing." Todd trudged down the hall and began cleaning. *Randy was right,* he thought. *Having Grandpa Willy come will be a pain.*

While he was finishing the bathtub, his sister Barb entered the room. "Won't it be neat to see Grandpa again? I remember helping him get eggs out of the chicken coop. I was always afraid to put my hands in the nest when the chickens were there, but you wouldn't remember that. You were too little."

"You're not much older than I am, so quit rubbing it in."

"I didn't mean to make you mad. Why are you so edgy?"

Todd frowned. "I'm not excited about Grandpa coming. It seems like we'll get more work."

"Todd, you're impossible! How would you feel if you were old and lonely?" Barb stormed out of the bathroom.

I certainly wouldn't make everybody take care of me, Todd thought, going to his room.

"Karen, Todd, Barb," his mother called, "Grandpa will arrive soon. Are your rooms picked up?" She stuck her head into Todd's bedroom. "Hurry and change clothes."

"Why do I have to get dressed up?"

"I want you to look nice."

As Todd put on his belt, the car pulled up. He watched as his father lifted a wheelchair out of the back. Grinning, Grandpa Willy slid into the wheelchair.

"Todd, hurry up," Barb said.

"I'm coming." Todd reached the kitchen door at the same time as Grandpa Willy.

"You've grown a lot." The old man spoke first. "Your father says you like to build things."

Todd looked at his grandfather's tan, thick forearms. "Yeah."

Grandpa Willy reached up to shake hands. "So do I."
Surprised by Grandpa Willy's strong grip, Todd squeezed harder.

"You grab the front, and I'll push," Mr. Stone said. "We'll have Grandpa Willy inside in no time."

"Dinner'll be ready in 10 minutes," Mrs. Stone said. "Wash up. Dad, Todd will show you where the bathroom is."

Todd began to push the wheelchair. "I'll do that," stated Grandpa Willy. "My legs aren't good," he said, rolling down the hall, "but I do what I can." He stopped. "Which door?"

"This one."

Grandpa Willy squeezed the wheelchair through with inches to spare.

Grandpa doesn't seem too bad yet, Todd thought. *I'm glad this bathroom is bigger than our other one.*

Minutes later Grandpa Willy wheeled into the kitchen. "Smells good, Caroline," he said, looking at Mrs. Stone. "I'll bet your cooking is still great."

Mrs. Stone laughed. "Wait and see, Dad. Todd, please call everyone to the table."

"Come and get it!" he shouted.

"Todd, that was uncalled for!" Mrs. Stone complained. "You should have gone to their rooms."

"I'm tired of doing that. Why can't they be ready?"

As Todd pulled out his chair, he noticed that Grandpa Willy was chuckling. "I used to shout to get everybody to dinner," Grandpa Willy quipped, "but that didn't work. So one day I got a cowbell and wailed the daylights out of it until my ears rang. Even neighbors came for dinner that night."

"That was on the farm," Mrs. Stone said quickly, trying to hide a smile.

Everyone sat down at the table. After Karen prayed, Todd asked, "Can I go to Randy's tomorrow morning? We want to enter a kite contest in Memorial Park on Sunday afternoon, and we have to build our kites."

"Sure," Mrs. Stone answered.

The next morning, Todd ate breakfast quickly and went to Randy's. "None of our books tell how to make kites," Randy said, "and Mom and Dad never built one."

"Maybe my father knows," Todd said.

Randy frowned. "Maybe we should forget the whole thing. We have to finish them by tonight."

"Let's ask my father anyway," Todd said.

"Aren't you supposed to be making kites?" Mr. Stone asked as the boys entered the living room.

"Yes, but we couldn't find directions on what to do and wondered if you knew."

Mr. Stone shook his head. "No."

"Hey, boys," Grandpa Willy said, "I can give you some pointers."

Randy stared at him. "Have you built a kite?"

"Sure." Grandpa Willy leaned forward. "Say, Bob, do you have a thin slat of wood like the kind on a crate? We also need fishing line, newspapers, glue, and rags for the tails."

"Hey boys," Grandpa Willy said, "I could give you some pointers."

Mr. Stone nodded.

Grandpa Willy took off his thick glasses. "Want me to show you how to build kites?"

"That'd be great!" Todd exclaimed.

Soon Todd and Randy had gathered the materials. "We're ready, Grandpa Willy."

"I'll be right there." Grandpa Willy laid down the newspaper and wheeled into the kitchen. "Will you help me get this contraption down this step?"

Randy grabbed the handles. "How long have you been in this?" he asked.

"Since September. I fell out of the apple tree and broke my hip."

"What do we do first?"

"Cut two long, narrow pieces off this slat." Randy and Todd carefully cut the strips. "Good. Now cut them here and here. The longer one is the vertical piece; the other is the horizontal one. Tie fishing line here," he added, pointing, "to hold them together."

"This is fun." Randy held up the frame.

Grandpa Willy laughed. "When I was your age, I made many kites." He pointed to the frame. "Cut a small slit on the ends of the sticks and string a fishing line around all four ends. Now get the line as tight as you can and tie a knot."

"Now what?" Randy asked.

"Lay the frame on top of a sheet of newspaper and cut around the outside edges, leaving about an inch extra. Good.

Now glue the edges over the fishing line. When the glue dries, the kite will be almost done."

"What's left?" Todd asked.

"This afternoon, tie a string across the crosspiece and make it bow up about three inches. Tie a string here and here, add a tail, and you'll be all set. We'll adjust the kites tonight, if the wind is good."

Just then Mr. and Mrs. Stone walked in. "I haven't seen a kite like this in years," Mr. Stone said.

"Thanks, Grandpa Willy," Randy said. "I didn't know people your age knew things like this. My grandpa forgets everything."

Grandpa Willy looked at Randy. "That's too bad. Not all older people are like that."

"Will you watch us fly our kites in the contest?" Todd asked.

"I'd love to." Grandpa Willy smiled and turned to Mr. Stone. "Would you drive me to the park tomorrow? I bet we've got a couple of winners."

Mr. Stone nodded. "I've known that all along."

Live It!

Many older people have wonderful experiences to share and are lots of fun, so get to know some of them when opportunities arise. Ask them questions and listen carefully. Yes, some older people have physical and mental challenges, but they aren't all like Randy's grandfather. Who knows? Maybe you'll end up with a new friend like Grandpa Willy who can do all kinds of things with you—maybe even kite building!

Read It!

"Do not cast me away when I am old; do not forsake me when my strength is gone."—Psalm 71:9

Pray About It!

Dear Lord, older people like Grandpa Willy do have lots of love and experiences to share with kids like me. I'd like to get to know more elderly people, so I ask you to make me aware of opportunities to meet them. There are probably older people nearby who get lonely and need some help, and I'd like to be their friend. Please fill me with your love so I have plenty to share.

*Whenever any family faces major changes, family
members feel uncomfortable at first. In this story, Bill
discovers that God uses a change that his family is
facing to bless everyone involved.*

But I Don't Want a New Father

As she entered the apartment, Mrs. Robbins dropped the
car keys into a small wicker basket.

"Have fun, Mom?" Billy stood outside his bedroom, wearing droopy, red pajamas.

"What're you doing up so late?" Mrs. Robbins sat on the
couch. "Yes, Mr. Peters and I had fun, Billy."

"Are you still going to marry him?"

"Yes."

Billy shuffled into the living room. "Why can't you wait?"

"I hoped you would feel differently about him now, after
all the things we've done together. Mr. Peters loves us a lot."

"But he's not like Dad." Billy crossed his arms. "Dad used to read in the evenings and do puzzles."

"I know," Mrs. Robbins said. "When I first met Mr. Peters at the church picnic, I didn't know I'd grow to love him."

"Well, I still don't love him." Billy stood up. "And I love you more than he does, and I don't want a new father." He ran into his bedroom and slammed the door.

Mrs. Robbins sighed. *I'll let him be by himself,* she thought, turning on a radio. *No, I want him to know how I feel, too.* She knocked on Billy's door. "Can we talk?"

"Yeah." The pillow muffled Billy's voice.

Mrs. Robbins sat on the edge of his bed. "Please look at me."

"You're going to marry him, and everything will change. But I want things to stay the same."

"There's nothing to talk about." Billy rolled over. "You're going to marry him, and everything will change. But I want things to stay the same."

"Many things change," she answered softly. "I know that you love me, and that means a lot. When your father died, our lives changed. I went back to work and couldn't spend as much time with you."

"But you've done things with me and my friends," Billy said. "Remember when we went tubing on the river?"

"Sure." Mrs. Robbins grinned. "When I met Mr. Peters, I didn't love him right away. It's not that I want you to have another father. It's . . ." She paused. "It's that I love him."

"I've tried to love him, Mom, but he's so different from Dad."

"Love doesn't happen all at once." Her eyes became moist. "I want you to be happy, too."

Billy stared at his mother. "Will you sing in the kitchen like you used to?"

Mrs. Robbins smiled weakly. "I didn't think you liked my singing."

"It's all right, most of the time."

"Let's finish talking about this tomorrow," Mrs. Robbins said as she shut the bedroom door.

The next morning, Billy's mother gently pushed on his shoulder. "Breakfast is ready."

"Uh-huh." When Billy entered the kitchen, cereal and

milk were on the table.

"How'd you sleep, Billy?"

"All right."

"I forgot to ask you about this." Mrs. Robbins held up a postcard. "It's about the Memorial Day father-son camp-out the church is having."

Billy took a bite. "Mr. Larson announced it in Sunday school."

"McCormick Woods is pretty. Are many of your friends going?"

"Some."

"Want to go?" Mrs. Robbins poured a cup of coffee.

"Don't know. I can't go anyway. Only boys with fathers can go."

"Are you sure?" Mrs. Robbins asked. "This card says an older adult can go in the father's place. I bet Mr. Peters would take you."

"I'd feel funny going with somebody who isn't my father."

"I'd feel funny going with somebody who isn't my father. And are you sure he'd take me?"

"Sure I'm sure. But do you want to go?"

"Yes."

"Mr. Peters loves the outdoors. He started to camp when he was your age."

"Will you ask him if he wants to go?"

"Sure," Mrs. Robbins answered. "You and he can rustle up equipment this week. The ferry will make one trip to the mainland at noon, as usual, and the bus will leave church at 10:00."

The next few days passed quickly. Billy cleaned out the basement, mowed the lawn, and fixed his bicycle. In the evenings, he read books on camping and piled camping clothes in his room.

Thursday evening, when Billy saw Mr. Peters walking up the sidewalk, he felt excited. Minutes later, his mother called. "Billy, Mr. Peters needs help."

Billy hurried to the living room. "Billy, I thought we'd better make sure we have what we'll need." Mr. Peters smiled. "I brought too much stuff, and we can't take it all."

"OK." They each made three trips to the truck and then sat in the living room.

"Should we take this?" Mr. Peters held up a propane lantern.

"No. I have a flashlight."

"That's the kind of thing I need to know." After sorting gear for almost two hours, they finally loaded up the truck.

"Well, we're done," Billy said.

"Thanks for your help."

"Are you hungry?" Mrs. Robbins brought in some chocolate chip cookies.

Billy ate three cookies. "What time will you pick me up?" he asked Mr. Peters.

"Nine o'clock."

"You've got a big day ahead, Billy," Mrs. Robbins said. "It's time for bed."

When Billy called, "Mom, I'm ready," his mother went into his bedroom. "Mom, Mr. Peters sure has neat stuff, doesn't he?"

"Yes, and he appreciated your help tonight. He says every camping trip is different." She kissed Billy goodnight and turned out the light. "I'll get the food ready. Tomorrow night you'll be in the tent."

When the sun's rays crept across the bedroom floor, Billy woke up. He put on his jeans and flannel shirt and tromped into the kitchen wearing unlaced hiking boots. As he finished breakfast, the doorbell rang and he jumped up. "I'm ready, Mr. Peters!" he exclaimed.

"Now all we need is the food," Mr. Peters said.

"I'll get it." Moments later Billy put the cooler into the truck.

"Don't forget to say good-bye to your mother."

They reached the church ten minutes early. When everything was loaded, the bus driver closed the storage door. "We're all set," he said, following Billy and Mr. Peters into the bus. The driver turned the key, but nothing happened. He tried again. Still nothing happened. "Can any of you fix a bus?" he joked.

"I can't even fix my car," someone replied, and several people laughed.

Mr. Peters walked down the aisle. "I'll try. Turn on your headlights." The driver pulled a switch, and Mr. Peters walked in front of the bus. "They're fine." He opened the hood. "The battery terminals look good." He reached under the dashboard and tinkered with the ignition switch. Nothing happened when he turned the key.

"What'll we do?" a boy asked. "We'll miss the ferry."

Mr. Peters examined something under the hood, and then crawled underneath. "I found it."

"Found what?" Billy heard the driver ask.

"A loose wire to the starter. Hand me that adjustable wrench." When the driver turned the key again, the engine started. Dusting off his pants, Mr. Peters closed the hood and climbed in.

As Mr. Peters started down the aisle, the boy in front of Billy turned around. "Is he your father? He sure knows lots about engines."

Billy grinned. "Not yet, but he soon will be." He moved over to give Mr. Peters more room.

Live It!

Many things happen to us that we can't control. Sometimes we face changes, like Billy, that make us uncomfortable and even afraid. But God understands how you feel and promises to be with you and listen to your prayers. The next time you feel afraid or uncertain, talk with God about it, too. After all, he wants you to experience his love and to guide you. He wants the best for you, and in return he asks for your obedience. As you learn to walk faithfully with him, he promises to give you awesome hope and peace.

Read It!

"For I know the plans I have for you," declares the LORD, "plans to prosper you and not to harm you, plans to give you hope and a future"—Jeremiah 29:11

Pray About It!

Dear Lord, you are in control of all things. Please help me to trust you more and to remember that you have special plans for me. Thanks for caring about how I feel and promising to give me hope and a future that I can look forward to. Help me to be willing to share my feelings with people I love and not let my feelings get all bottled up inside me.

When someone in your school keeps trying to make your life miserable, it's not easy to respond back in a loving way. In this story, Justin faces this situation and makes a choice that leads to a surprising result.

Anyone but Him!

Justin Parker got up from the dining room table and laid down his book. "Mom," he asked, "can I still go fishing? My homework's done for Monday."

"It's getting colder," his mother replied, "and I heard on the radio it might snow heavily."

"Aw, Mom, I've been trying since summer to catch that trout. Soon the pond'll freeze over."

Mrs. Parker smiled. "OK. Have everything you need? And Mollie will want to go." Hearing her name, the German shepherd sat up and cocked her ears.

"My backpack is still full of survival gear from my trip with Dad in the wilderness area," Justin said, adding a sandwich and a water bottle.

Minutes later, he walked down the hill behind the house and took the winding, little-used trail toward Pinion Canyon. "Today's the day, Mollie," he exclaimed. "That fish is mine!"

Mollie walked beside him, breathing out small puffs of mist.

Large snowflakes began to fall. *The weather's going to be bad,* Justin thought, *but I'm not quitting yet.* He put on his raincoat over his jacket and speeded up his pace. Careful not to step on loose rocks, he worked his way slowly over fallen trees and around boulders that tumbled long ago from the shadowy cliffs above.

As Justin neared the first small valley, Mollie suddenly stopped to listen. "What do you hear?" Justin asked. Then he heard it, too—a cry coming from a steep, wooded ravine.

Mollie whined and headed for the sound, stopping only long enough for Justin to catch up. "How are we going to get that fish if we go the wrong way?" he asked aloud.

The snow was falling in larger flakes; the wind began to bend the thinner aspen trees. Again Justin heard the muffled cry. Mollie ran ahead, barking.

"I'm coming," Justin shouted, forcing his way through thick scrub oak. Branches caught at his raincoat. His heart pounded from the climb.

As he rounded a bend, Justin saw a rock wall about twenty-five feet ahead. A boy sat underneath an overhang. *Oh no! Not Michael Edwards!* Justin thought. *I'm so tired of him picking on me since we moved here just because I can't skate.*

As Justin walked closer, he saw that Michael's face was twisted with pain. "We heard you back in the creek bed," Justin said. "What happened?"

Michael squirmed. "I went hiking and fell off the ledge hours ago. My knee got hurt. Nobody knows I'm out here. I just kept yelling." His words were strained, and he shivered.

"Let's see if you can walk," Justin said. "I'll make a crutch."

"Out of what?" Michael moaned.

Justin removed a lightweight hatchet from his backpack and soon had chopped off a limb and all but one branch. "Try this," he said, handing the limb to Michael. "How does it feel? Here, cushion your armpit with this hat and put on this warm sweater."

"Thanks." For a second Michael's face softened, then he asked, "How do you suggest I get home, genius? Run all the way with a bum knee?"

Justin ignored the sarcasm and brushed snow off his glasses. "I'll steady you."

They began to ease their way down the ravine. The snow-covered rocks and deadfall were slippery, and Michael nearly fell several times. Only Justin's steady grip kept Michael on his feet.

"Here, take my gloves," Justin said.

"Isn't that your only pair?" Michael asked.

"My extra socks will make pretty good gloves."

"Where'd you learn all this outdoor stuff?"

"I backpack with my father a lot. Maybe it's not quite as cool as skateboarding, but I enjoy it."

Michael hung his head. "Nobody ever taught me things about the woods."

Suddenly Michael's left foot flew out from under him,

causing both of them to fall. The crutch cracked.

"Are you OK?" Justin asked.

"I guess so, but the crutch is history."

Justin helped Michael stand up. "Put your arm around my shoulder." Snow pelted their faces as they walked, arm in arm.

After hobbling about five more minutes, Michael bit his lip to keep from crying out in pain. "I can't go any farther," he said. "What'll we do? We've got so far to go."

"You'll be OK." Justin guided him alongside a large fallen tree, then pulled out a large piece of nylon. "Stay here, out of the wind. Put this around you." Using dead branches and a small candle, Justin started a fire to keep Michael warm.

"I have to get going. Wait here so we can find you."

As the wind increased, Justin felt a chill go down his back. "I have to get going. Wait here so we can find you." Mollie shook off a layer of snow and nuzzled Michael.

"Hey, be careful, OK?"

"No problem. Mollie'll get me home." As Justin began

walking, cold air whipped his cheeks; his fingers and ears grew colder. Even with the flashlight, he could barely see the trail. Several times he checked his compass.

After what seemed like forever, Justin reached a rock outcropping he had climbed in July. Moments later, he saw the glow of lights from his house.

"Well, if you aren't a sight!" his mother exclaimed, giving him a big hug as soon as he entered the door. "We were about ready to send out a search party," she teased. Justin's father grinned and put down his boots. Mollie shook herself; water and snow flew everywhere.

"I left Michael up there," Justin blurted out. "He can't walk."

"Whoa . . . slow down," Mr. Parker said. "You mean, the Michael who lives up the street?"

Justin quickly described what had happened, then Mr. Parker called the county sheriff. "I'll come with you," Justin heard his father say. "I know where Michael is."

"Can I go?" Justin asked.

"No, you've already had quite a day. Stay here and get warm. We'll find Michael pretty quickly."

After ten o'clock, Mr. Parker called from the hospital. "Michael will be fine, but it was tough getting him down."

The next morning, Mrs. Parker handed Justin the phone. "It's for you."

"Hey, dude, it's me, Michael. The doctor said I badly strained the ligaments in my knee. But after I heal up, I'll show you how to skate. And will you teach me some outdoor things?"

"Sure." Justin smiled as he hung up the phone. *Maybe the rest of this school year won't be as hard as I thought.*

Live It!

It's easy to be kind to kids who like you. But what about being kind to kids who *don't* like you? That's a lot tougher, but that's exactly what God wants you to do. God wants each of us to share his love with *everybody*.

Read It!

"So in everything, do to others what you would have them do to you."—Matthew 7:12

Pray About It!

Lord, change my attitude toward people who have been unkind to me. Help me to love them the way you love them and to always be kind. I can't do it on my own. I want them to realize you can make a big difference in their lives, too.

Here's what I think...

Skate Park Swap

91

Here's what I think...

Here's what I think...

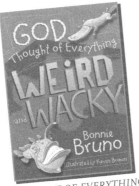